The Thirsty Moose is based on a traditional
Native American story

First published 2004
Evans Brothers Limited
2A Portman Mansions
Chiltern St
London WIU 6NR

British Library Cataloguing in Publication Data
Orme, David
    The thirsty moose. - (Zig zags)
    1. Moose - Juvenile fiction 2. Children's stories
    I. Title
    823. 9'14 [J]

ISBN 0237527928

Printed in China by WKT Company Limited

Series Editor: Louise John
Design: Robert Walster
Production: Jenny Mulvanny
Series Consultant: Gill Matthews

ZIG ZAG

The Thirsty Moose

by David Orme

illustrated by Mike Gordon

Evans

Big Moose was thirsty.

He went to the river and
drank and drank.

The water went down
and down.

"Stop it!" shouted the beaver.
"My home will be spoiled!"

But Big Moose wouldn't listen.

10

"Stop it!" shouted the
muskrat.
"I'll have nowhere to swim!"

Big Moose still
wouldn't listen.

"Stop it!" bubbled the fish.
"We can't live without
water!"

Big Moose still wouldn't listen.

"Stop it!" buzzed the fly.
"Or I'll fight you!"

Big Moose listened this time.

"Go on," said Big Moose.
"I dare you!"

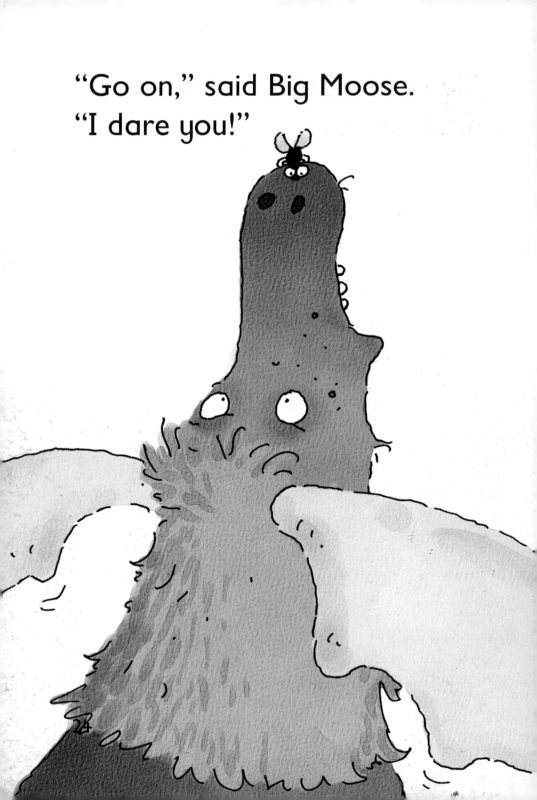

Big Moose started
drinking again.

The fly flew into Big Moose's ear.

"I'll teach you not to listen!"
he buzzed. Then he started
to bite.

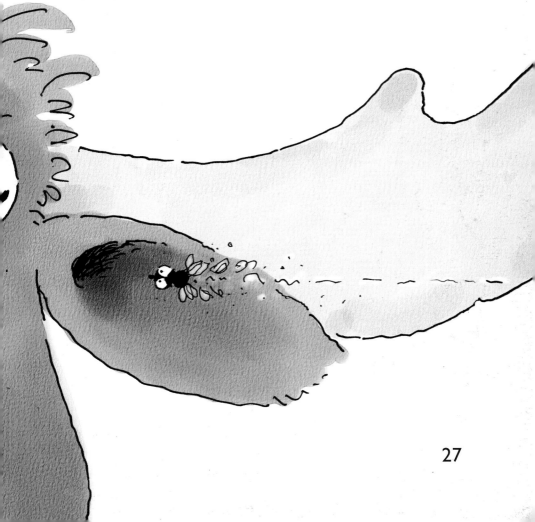

"Stop it!" shouted Big Moose.

But the fly didn't stop.
Big Moose ran away
as fast as he could.

He never came back
to the river again!

Why not try reading another ZigZag book?

Dinosaur Planet   ISBN: 0 237 52667 0
by David Orme and Fabiano Fiorin

Tall Tilly   ISBN: 0 237 52668 9
by Jillian Powell and Tim Archbold

Batty Betty's Spells   ISBN: 0 237 52669 7
by Hilary Robinson and Belinda Worsley

The Thirsty Moose   ISBN: 0 237 52666 2
by David Orme and Mike Gordon

The Clumsy Cow   ISBN: 0 237 52656 5
by Julia Moffatt and Lisa Williams

Open Wide!   ISBN: 0 237 52657 3
by Julia Moffatt and Anni Axworthy